Bank Street Ready-to-Read™

Follow
That Fish

by Joanne Oppenheim
Illustrated by Devis Grebu

A Byron Preiss Book

A BANTAM LITTLE ROOSTER BOOK
NEW YORK · TORONTO · LONDON · SYDNEY · AUCKLAND

I had a fish
on my line.
And that big fish
was almost mine!

I reeled him out.
I reeled him in.
I really nearly
touched his fin.

But then, he gave
a mighty spin,
snapped my line,
and pulled me in!

I went down deep.
I went down fast.
I went down past
a sunken mast.

I met an eel
with beady eyes,
who looked at me
with some surprise.

His mouth was big.
His mouth was wide.
His big wide mouth
had spots INSIDE.

He looked at me
as if to say,
"This place is mine!
Now go away!"

I would not argue
with an eel.
I did not care
to be his meal.

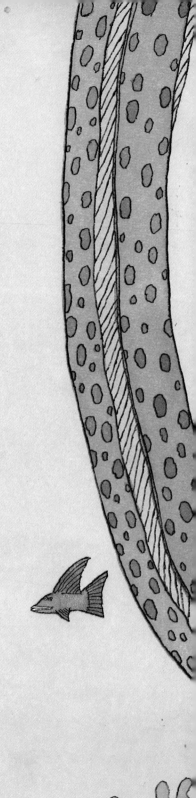

I saw a jug,
a place to hide.
Could my big fish
be there inside?

I poked my arm
inside the jug,
and my arm got
an eight-leg hug.

It did not hurt.
She meant no harm.
She only wished
to hold my arm!

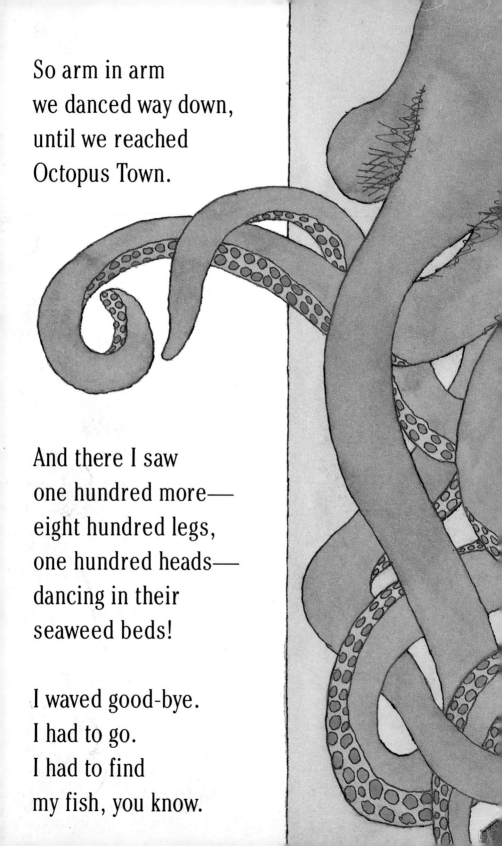

So arm in arm
we danced way down,
until we reached
Octopus Town.

And there I saw
one hundred more—
eight hundred legs,
one hundred heads—
dancing in their
seaweed beds!

I waved good-bye.
I had to go.
I had to find
my fish, you know.

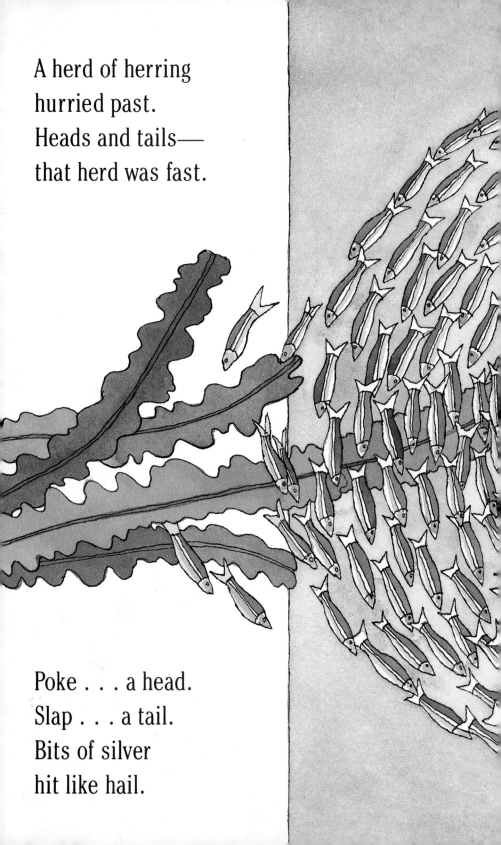

A herd of herring
hurried past.
Heads and tails—
that herd was fast.

Poke . . . a head.
Slap . . . a tail.
Bits of silver
hit like hail.

By then I felt
it might be best
to stop awhile
and take a rest.

I found a seat.
A big brown rock.
When I sat down,
I had a *shock.*

The rock took off
with me on top!

A turtle took me riding!
He took me nice and slow.
A turtle took me gliding
to where the flatfish grow!

Ten flatfish flipped
and flopped a lot.
Each flatfish had
two eyes on top.

First they flip,
and then they flop.
They flip to see
where they should drop.

My fish was fat.
He was not flat.
He was not here,
and that was that!

Then up we went.
We did not stop.
We really nearly
reached the top.

Past the striped fish.
Past the pipe fish.
Past the checkered
red-and-white fish.

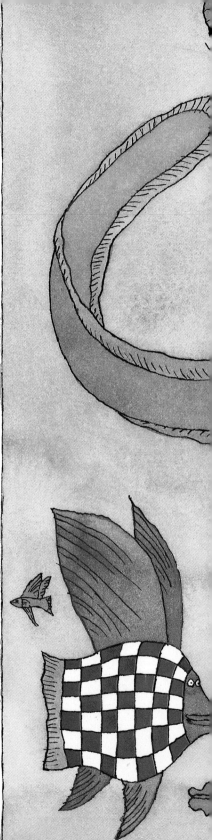

I held on tight.
At least, I tried.
But then . . . I slipped!
I lost my ride.

Down . . .
    Down . . .
        Down . . .
            I could not stop!

Down . . .
    Down . . .
        Down . . .
            What a drop!

I dropped so deep,
so far below,
I found myself
where darkfish glow!

Small bright lights
winked on each head.
Their head lights glowed
in green and red!

I never wished
to go so low.
So far deep down
where fishes glow.

I rushed to leave
the glowing dark.
But
going up . . .

I saw—
a SHARK!

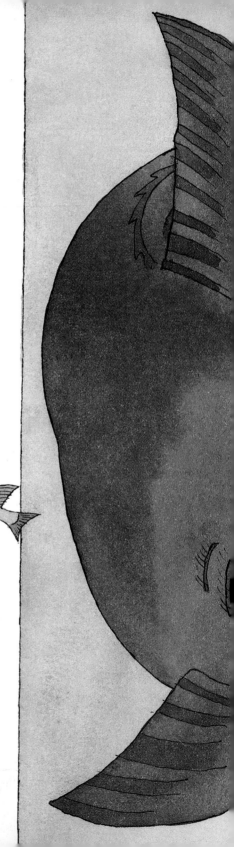

His eyes were green
and wild and mean.
A meaner fish
I've never seen.

And then and there
I had a wish.
I did not wish
to catch my fish.

And there and then
I wished instead
that I was home . . .
quite safe in bed!

And there I was.
I got my wish!
I woke up . . .
without my fish.

Joanne Oppenheim is the author of more than two dozen picture books, including *Have You Seen Birds?,* which won the National Picture Book of the Year Award in Canada. A former elementary school teacher, she is co-author of *Choosing Books for Kids* and is currently a Senior Editor for the Bank Street College Media Group. Ms. Oppenheim divides her time between New York City and her home in Monticello, New York.

Devis Grebu was born in Romania and educated at the Academy of Fine Arts in Bucharest. He has illustrated more than thirty books in German, French, and English and has also created designs for theater sets, costumes, and stamps. Mr. Grebu has won several awards for his work, including the Sydney Taylor Book Award. He has lived in Israel and France and now resides outside of New York City.